Sofie & Daniel

Get Ready for

Earthquakes

Written by Lin Glen

Illustrated by Darcy Brown

This book is dedicated to my niece Sofie, my nephew Daniel, my grandchildren James and Zoe, and to all children and families in earthquake country.

Special thanks to expert reviewers Troy Nicolini and Jim Falls, to my technical advisor Jonathan Glen, and to my husband David.

And many thanks to: Seth; Jesse, Laura, and James; Sofia; Janet; Heather, Mat, Silas, and Asa; Emily, Trevor, and Elsa; Tamara; Connie; Paula, Stasia, and Heather; Robert; Karen; Jon; Lori; Michelle; Pat; Lisken, Soren, and Eero; my Aunt Alyce; and to everyone else who's given me help, encouragement, and advice.

Book layout and design by Amy Barnes, Persimmon Graphics

www.sofieanddaniel.com

ISBN 978-0-9975928-0-1

Keywords: earthquake safety; earthquake preparedness; earthquake safety for kids; earthquake safety for families; emergency preparedness; earthquake safety kit; preparing for earthquakes; earthquakes children; earthquake facts children

Are you ready?

"What's happening?" cried Daniel.

"What?" said Sofie sleepily. "I was dreaming I was on a boat and it was going up and down – hey, what's happening?"

"Help!" said Daniel. "It's raining stuffies!"

Mommy and Daddy ran into their room.

"We had an earthquake," said Daddy. "Where's Daniel? Hey buddy, are you OK? Give me a hug."

"What if something heavier had been on that shelf?" said Mommy. "Daniel could have been hurt! That's it! We're going to get ready for earthquakes."

"Will an earthquake happen again?" asked Daniel.

"We might feel some smaller ones – they're called 'aftershocks,'" said Daddy.

"I remembered what to do when an earthquake happens!" said Sofie excitedly. "Drop, cover, and hold on! We learned that at school! Get on your knees under a table, get really small, put your hand over the back of your neck, and hold onto the table."[1]

[1] See Parents' Notes on page 30 for what to do "During an Earthquake"

"I feel an aftershock happening right now!" said Sofie.

"I think that's just a passing truck, but let's practice like it was another earthquake," said Mommy. "OK, everyone – drop, cover, and hold on!"

"AH-CHOO!!!" Daddy sneezed. "We need to dust more often."

"Daddy!" said Daniel, "That felt like another earthquake!"

After breakfast; Sofie, Daniel, and Mommy got into their van. "Where are we going, Mommy?" asked Sofie.

"I have the day off from work so we can talk to the earthquake scientists at the university — Dr. Terra and Dr. Petra," said Mommy. "I've seen them on TV."

"Hi folks," said Dr. Petra. "We heard you were stopping by. What did you think of that earthquake? It was a real rock-and-roller!"

"I was scared," said Sofie. "I dreamt I was in a boat that went up and down and then Daniel got covered in stuffies – for real!"

"What are those things over there?" asked Daniel.

"These are machines that help us to measure earthquakes, Daniel," said Dr. Petra. "This one is called a seismograph (pronounced SIZE-mo-graf)."

Dr. Terra said, "The seismograph has a needle that writes on paper when an earthquake happens, so we can see how big it was."

"If I jump really, really hard – like this," said Sofie, "will the machine show an earthquake?"

"Sorry, Sofie. You're not heavy enough to make an earthquake this seismograph would show," said Dr. Petra, laughing.

"Why do we even HAVE earthquakes?" asked Daniel. [2]

"The earth is always moving a little bit, way under the ground," said Dr. Terra. "Sometimes things on top of the ground shake a little, too, and we call that an earthquake. Most earthquakes are small and we can't feel them."

"Can't scientists stop them?" Daniel asked.

"No, but we can learn about them to find out how to make buildings safer when earthquakes do happen," said Dr. Petra. "And we can show people how to keep themselves safer, too."

"Uh oh, where's Sofie?" asked Mommy.

[2] See Parents' Notes on page 30 for "Does your child have more questions?"

"Here I am," said Sofie. "Look, Dr. Terra! I know how to stay safe in an earthquake."

"Well done, Sofie!" said Dr. Terra. "Practicing 'drop, cover, and hold on' is really important. Don't ever run outside, if you do, things could fall on you."

"But what if an earthquake happens again when I'm sleeping?" asked Sofie.

"Stay where you are, put your pillow over your head and neck, and wait until the shaking stops," said Dr. Terra. "And, keep shoes and a flashlight under your bed to protect your feet in case there's broken glass on the floor."

"Once I saw some buildings on TV that fell down from an earthquake," said Daniel.

"That sometimes happens in countries that don't have laws to make buildings earthquake-safe," said Dr. Terra. "Our country does have laws like that. And you can make your house even safer."

"I want to know more about that," said Mommy.

"One more thing," said Dr. Terra. "Tsunamis (pronounced soo-NAH-meez) happen when a BIG earthquake or a BIG landslide or eruption under the ocean makes REALLY BIG waves that come far up onto the land."

Dr. Petra said, "If you're at the beach and:

– you feel an earthquake that's longer than 20 seconds, OR
– you hear a VERY LOUD ocean roar, OR
– the water goes out really, really far and you can see the ocean floor

you should move to higher ground or go inland as quickly as you can and stay there until officials say it's safe to return." [3]

[3] See Parents' Notes on page 30 for ways to get the Tsunami Safety Checklist

"Here are booklets about earthquake and tsunami safety," said Dr. Terra. "Some are from the Red Cross."

"Thanks!" said Mommy. "I wondered where I could get that information." [4]

"And today's your lucky day," said Dr. Petra. "We're giving you an earthquake safety starter kit. It has straps to secure your TV and bookshelves, a tool to turn off your gas and water, and a home safety poster."

"Thanks!" said Sofie over her shoulder as she ran out the door.

"This Earthquake Safety Checklist from Dr. Terra will help us get ready for earthquakes quickly," said Mommy as they drove home. "Daddy's coming home from work early so we can do it today." *

* See page 36 for your copy

"Guess what, Daddy?" said Sofie. "We went to see the earthquake scientists! They showed us the earthquake measuring machines and everything."

"And they gave us these booklets that tell us what to do to be safe," said Daniel.

"Awesome!" said Daddy. "Let's make a game plan and we'll all work together to get this done."

"You guys start reading the checklist and tell us how to get ready for earthquakes while I make lunch," said Daddy.

"OK, it says here that we need to make emergency kits for home, work, and for the kids," said Mommy

"Can we make our own emergency kits right now?" asked Sofie.

"Oh no!" said Daniel. "Quick – we have to drop, cover, and hold on!"

"My favorite vase!" said Mommy, with tears in her eyes.

 "I'm scared!" cried Sofie.

"Well done, guys! We remembered to drop, cover, and hold on. The aftershock stopped and we're okay – but the vase isn't. Sorry, honey," said Daddy. "Now let's get back to work. I'm going to make sure everything in the house is okay, too. Kids – go upstairs and find something to put your emergency kits in." [5]

[5] See Parents' Notes on page 30 for "How to help your child recover after a large earthquake"

"Look, Mommy – we found our old school backpacks," said Daniel.

"Great!" said Mommy. "What do you want to put in them? You need enough for three days."

"Water!" said Sofie.

"Food," said Daniel, "and socks and a shirt and stuff."

"Underpants!" said Sofie, giggling.

"Silly," said Mommy, "but you're right. Go get your extra clothes and remember to get a little stuffed earthquake buddy too. I'll get the water and food."

PARENTS, KNOW YOUR CHILD'S SCHOOL EMERGENCY PLAN

Make a personal/school emergency kit together with each child: Into a small backpack, large zip-top bag, or similar container marked with the child's name, put at least: 3 small bottles of water; 3 granola bars or similar snacks; small flashlight or "glow stick"; extra set of clothes; whistle; pocket-sized packs of tissues and sanitizing wipes; small pack of adhesive bandages; small stuffed "earthquake buddy"; recent photo of the child with parents; emergency contact info. Tell the child's teacher about "must-have" medicines or prescriptions. Extras: space blanket, toothbrush and toothpaste, comforting letter from parents to child, game, toy, art supplies.

"We finished our emergency kits," said Daniel proudly.

"Well done," said Daddy. "Let's see what you put in there."

"Look Daddy," said Sofie, "Tigie is going to be my little stuffed earthquake buddy."

"Now let's fill out the Family Emergency Plan form," said Mommy. "Who should we call out of town to tell them we're safe?"

"Aunt Kimmie," said Daniel. "Daddy says she's always talking about people on the phone."

"I meant that in a good way," said Daddy quickly. "Let's fill out these emergency plan cards, too." [6]

[6] See Parents' Notes on page 30 for "Make a family emergency plan and cards"

"Now, let's make our home emergency kit," said Mommy. "Daniel, you get a flashlight and Sofie, you get a can opener."

"Here's the can opener," said Sofie. "Let's open some cans!"

"Sofie! It's for emergencies," said Daniel.

"There are some things on the list that we don't have, like a battery radio and extra water. I'll get them this afternoon," said Mommy. "I want our emergency kits to be finished today!"

PARENTS – MAKE A FAMILY EMERGENCY KIT WITH THINGS LIKE:
AT LEAST 3 days of water (1 gallon per person per day), first-aid kit, AT LEAST 3 days' supply of canned food and other food that doesn't need water for prep, supply of cash in small bills, flashlights, can opener, necessary medications, battery-powered radio, batteries, emergency blankets, multi-tool, personal hygiene supplies, copy of family emergency plan and cards, (see pages 38 and 39) *

* For more ideas, see pp. 32 and 33

"Here's a poster Dr. Terra gave us about fixing dangerous things in our house," said Daniel. "Can we fix our house now?"

"Yes," said Mommy. "You and Daddy can take it with you and fix the things that could fall in an earthquake, like bookshelves or the TV. We might have another aftershock."

"The TV could fall?" asked Daddy. "The basketball playoffs start tomorrow! Let's get it done!" [7]

"We want to help!" said Sofie and Daniel.

"OK, kids. Sofie, you hold the screws while I attach these bookshelves to the wall," said Daddy. "Daniel, you can hold the ladder for me while I move the shelf that's over your bed. I don't want anything else falling on you guys in an earthquake." [8]

(Parents – many types of furniture strap systems are available. Make sure the ones you get are flexible.)

[8] See Parents' Notes on page 30 for "How to secure things that could fall in an earthquake"

27

"It feels so good to be ready for earthquakes," said Mommy. "We put our emergency kits together and things are strapped down in the house. Sofie and Daniel, what did you learn today?"

"I remembered how to drop, cover, and hold on if an earthquake happens," said Sofie. "And I learned not to run outside. See the picture I made to remind us to practice?"

"I learned how to fix things so they won't fall on you, like shelves and the TV," said Daniel.

"We have a few more things left to do. I made a list and we'll finish this weekend, but we worked hard today," said Daddy. "Let's have ice cream and play some games to celebrate!"

"Yay!" said Sofie and Daniel.

That night, when Sofie and Daniel went to bed, Sofie asked, "were you scared from the earthquakes, Daniel?"

"A little," said Daniel. "But not so much now, because we made our room safe with Daddy and we made our emergency kits with Mommy. G'night, Sofie."

"G'night, Daniel," said Sofie.

After they fell asleep, Sofie and Daniel both dreamt they were earthquake scientists, helping people stay safe when earthquakes happen.

PARENTS' NOTES

1 (from page 6) **DURING AN EARTHQUAKE**

WITH INFANT OR SMALL CHILD: Protect them with your body. **Infant**: hold the baby to your chest as you drop, cover, and hold on. **Small child**: crouch over the child or pull them next to you and hold them close with one arm as you drop, cover, and hold on.

INSIDE: Stay where you are. DROP to the ground, take COVER under something large like a table or in an inside corner of the room away from glass or things that could fall on you, put a hand over your neck and head, HOLD ON to whatever you're under.

OUTSIDE: Stay there – away from buildings, power lines, streetlights and things that could fall on you.

WHILE DRIVING: Stop when it's safe – away from buildings, overpasses, or power lines. Stay in the vehicle. After a large earthquake, don't drive on bridges, overpasses, or ramps that could be damaged.

Also see: www.ready.gov/earthquakes

2 (from page 10) **DOES YOUR CHILD HAVE MORE QUESTIONS?**

If your child has questions about earthquakes that you can't answer, call: Science Information Services (SIS) to speak to a scientist – toll-free 1-888-ASK-USGS (1-888-275-8747) then Press 2 **Also see:** www.usgs.gov and search for "Ask a Geologist"

3 (from page 13) **FOR A COPY OF THE RED CROSS READY TSUNAMI SAFETY CHECKLIST**

Call the Red Cross at: 1-800-RED-CROSS (1-800-733-2767) and ask for the Tsunami Safety Checklist.
Also see: www.redcross.org and search for Red Cross Ready Tsunami Safety Checklist

4 (from page 14) **FOR INFORMATION ON PREPARING FOR EARTHQUAKES:**

See the "Earthquake Safety Checklist" on page 36. Or call the Red Cross at 1-800 RED CROSS (1-800-733-2767), Press 6 for the local office, and ask for the brochure "Get a kit. Make a plan. Be informed", available in English and Spanish.
Also see: http://www.ready.gov/earthquakes and click on "before" and "after" tabs – information in eleven languages.

5 (from page 19) **HOW TO HELP YOUR CHILD RECOVER AFTER A LARGE EARTHQUAKE**

- Listen – answer questions, give your child factual information – not too much – let them lead.
- Keep calm and carry on – your child will learn how to deal with earthquakes from you.
- Teach your child to be prepared, tell them what you've done, let them help the family prepare.
- Limit TV and video time. Video and TV earthquake coverage can be scary for children and teens.
- Help your child return to normal activities like school, sports, and playgroups.
- Changes in a child's sleeping, eating, and other behaviors can mean they're upset. Find professional counseling if they don't stop. (also see: www.ready.gov search for: earthquakes parents coping)

6 (from page 23) **MAKE A FAMILY EMERGENCY PLAN AND CARDS**

Use the forms at the back of this book - pages 38-39.
Also see: www.ready.gov/earthquakes "Before an Earthquake" and then click on "Family Emergency Communication Plan".

7 (from page 26) **MAKE YOUR HOME EARTHQUAKE SAFE**

See Earthquake Home Hazard Hunt poster on page 35. For phone # to order one, see FEMA on p. 31.
Also see: www.fema.gov and search for Earthquake Home Hazard Hunt. (Print horizontally or "landscape")

8 (from page 27) **HOW TO SECURE THINGS THAT COULD FALL IN AN EARTHQUAKE**

Ask for flexible earthquake furniture and appliance safety straps at your local hardware store. Follow the package instructions for attaching them to the wall.
Also see: http://earthquakecountry.org . Click on "Prepare" and then "Secure your Space".

FOR MORE HELP AND INFORMATION

American Red Cross
For booklets on earthquake preparedness (ask for the brochure "Earthquake Safety Checklist" available in English and Spanish), earthquake recovery, and first aid: http://www.redcross.org/prepare/disaster/earthquake
Phone: 1-800-RED CROSS (1-800-733-2767) press 6

Earthquake Country Alliance
"Living on Shaky Ground" and "Putting Down Roots in Earthquake Country" – highly recommended earthquake/tsunami booklets in English and Spanish plus other earthquake preparedness information and booklets. Booklets are available for organizations and for northern and southern California, Oregon, Utah, Nevada, Alaska, and the Central U.S.. http://www.earthquakecountry.org select RESOURCES.
Phone: the ECA Information Line at 1-213-740-3262

Emergency Kit Content Lists
All of the agencies on this page have suggested emergency kit lists. Call them or go to their websites.

FEMA (Federal Emergency Management Agency) Ready.gov
Earthquake preparedness and recovery information, forms, Home Hazard Hunt poster, and more – some information available in 11 languages: http://www.ready.gov/earthquakes
Phone: (FEMA Ready.gov publications warehouse) 1-800-237-3239 – press 1

"Totally Unprepared"
Slightly ironic "how to" earthquake preparedness videos and other information – a project of the California Governor's Office of Emergency Services, the California Earthquake Authority, and the California Seismic Safety Commission
http://www.totallyunprepared.com/wps/get-ready-quick/ (no phone number)

Tsunami Safety Checklist
Go to redcross.org, type "tsunami safety checklist" in search box, click "disaster safety library", scroll to "tsunami", select "tsunami safety checklist" – also available in Spanish.
Phone: 1-707-443-0574 ext. 222 – Northwest California Tsunami Program Manager, National Weather Service for brochure – "How to Survive a Tsunami"

United States Geological Survey
Information for kids, preparedness handbook, scientific information.
http://earthquake.usgs.gov/learn/preparedness.php
Phone: 1-888-ASK-USGS (1-888-275-8747), Select Option 2

Home Emergency Supply Kit Ideas

Water - (1 gallon per person per day for at least 3-5 days) include bleach to purify it if needed: 1/8 teaspoon unscented bleach per gallon of water (mix, wait 30 minutes or more to drink)

Food - (enough to feed your family for at least 3-5 days.) Choose foods that are easily stored, ready-to-eat, shelf life of at least 12 months, and take no water to prepare. Include canned foods like soups, stews, fruit, canned juice, and packaged milk, peanut butter, etc. If you must have noodles or rice, include packaged broth.

Cooking supplies - a way to cook, like a grill or camp stove and fuel; pot and/or pan; utensils; disposable paper plates, cups, utensils; manual can opener; foil and plastic wrap/bags; waterproof matches; and garbage bags

Clothing - (a complete change of clothes for each person – heavy enough to protect from cold and stored to stay dry and clean), comfortable boots or heavy shoes, hats, gloves, and rain ponchos

Safety supplies - battery lantern, flashlight, portable radio, extra batteries, candles and waterproof matches, duct tape, good scissors, whistles (to get attention and keep track of kids), rope, sharp knife, small tools like utility turn-off wrench, and fire extinguisher

General supplies - cash in small bills and quarters; pencil and paper; city/area maps; extra house/car keys, ID cards for everyone; space blankets; emergency contacts/reunification plan; and insurance information

Hygiene supplies - waterless soap and hand sanitizer, sanitizing wipes, liquid detergent, shampoo, toothbrush and toothpaste, tissues, toilet paper, contractor-weight trash bags (for human waste), paper towels, sanitary supplies (sanitary pads make great pressure bandages)

Medical supplies - first aid kit (purchase or make your own), first aid book, medications and extra eyeglasses plus prescriptions for each, and a list of medical providers

For evacuation - tent, sleeping bags, wheeled trash cans or duffels to move supplies, cards and/or games

Special items - for infants, children, elderly, disabled

For pets - proof of rabies vaccination, leashes, water, food, carriers or shelter.

Adapted from the SF Fire Department
Neighborhood Emergency Response Teams supplies lists
For other examples of emergency kit lists
go to ready.gov/kit

Workplace Kit

A simple kit that will help you to get to your home or reunification site:

Comfortable walking shoes
Flashlight/headlamp
Portable radio
Small amount of water/food
Cash in small bills/quarters
Family contact information, local maps
Personal hygiene kit
Proof of home address, like a utility bill with street address

▶ **Do you know your employer's plans for evacuation? Sheltering in place? Contacting you after a disaster?**

Car Kit

Same items as Workplace Kit plus backpack with:

First aid kit
Flares
Change of clothes

▶ **Never let your gas tank get below half a tank. Gas pumps need power, roads to gas station may be impassable.**

Kits for Kids

Contact information for Mom and Dad, plus out-of-state contact

Identification with your names and contact numbers

Who is authorized to pick up your kids if you can't?

Family reunification plan with a note from Mom and Dad that everything will be all right.

Favorite book or toy especially for younger kids

Favorite snacks and juice boxes

Change of clothes

Extra medication stored safely with the school

Same time every year (pick a date you'll remember):

▶ **Check and rotate water, food, batteries, clothes**

▶ **Use or donate food about to expire to Food Banks**

► Are You Ready?

Kids – are you ready to put your own earthquake emergency kit together?
Get a small backpack, ziptop bag, or other small container and start!
Put a check mark next to each item after you put it into your kit:

 ❑ WATER

 ❑ TISSUES

 ❑ GRANOLA BARS

 ❑ WIPES

 ❑ FLASHLIGHT OR GLOW STICK

 ❑ BANDAGES

 ❑ EXTRA SET OF CLOTHES

 ❑ QUAKE BUDDY

 ❑ FAMILY PHOTO

 ❑ WHISTLE

 ❑ TOOTHBRUSH AND TOOTHPASTE

 ❑ ART SUPPLIES OR GAMES

 ❑ EMERGENCY CONTACT CARD

Well done! Now you have your own earthquake emergency kit.
Keep it at home where you can grab it fast, or take it to school.

Earthquake Home Hazard Hunt

Detailed recommendations for reducing earthquake hazards in your home are on the FEMA website. See page 31.

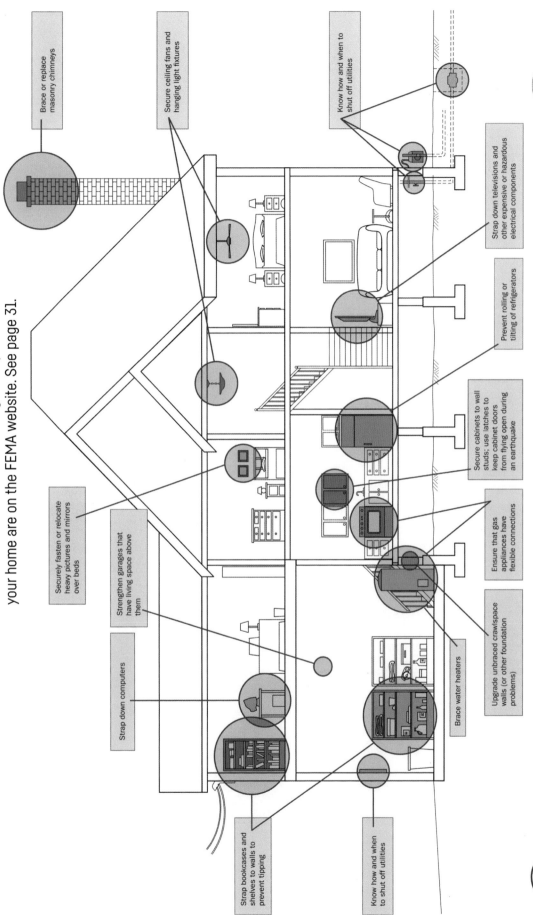

Brace or replace masonry chimneys

Secure ceiling fans and hanging light fixtures

Know how and when to shut off utilities

Strap down televisions and other expensive or hazardous electrical components

Prevent rolling or tilting of refrigerators

Secure cabinets to wall studs; use latches to keep cabinet doors from flying open during an earthquake

Ensure that gas appliances have flexible connections

Upgrade unbraced crawlspace walls (or other foundation problems)

Brace water heaters

Know how and when to shut off utilities

Strap bookcases and shelves to walls to prevent tipping

Strap down computers

Strengthen garages that have living space above them

Securely fasten or relocate heavy pictures and mirrors over beds

nehrp

FEMA

EARTHQUAKE SAFETY CHECKLIST
SPEND 1 MINUTE TO FINISH PREPARING

PROTECT YOUR FAMILY

	Yes	No
Have you practiced **"Drop, Cover, and Hold On"** with your family?	O	O
Do you have a **home emergency kit** with a radio, and a **3 day supply of food and water per person?**	O	O
Does each family member have **an emergency wallet card?**	O	O

PROTECT YOUR KIDS

	Yes	No
Do you know what your children's **school disaster plan** is?	O	O
Do your kids have **personal emergency backpacks** with shoes, a flashlight, water, copies of their ID, snacks, and a toy?	O	O

PROTECT YOUR FAMILY

	Yes	No
Are your **framed photos** hung with **earthquake-safe hooks?**	O	O
Are your **computer monitors** secured to the desk with straps?	O	O
Is your **television** secured with **straps?**	O	O
Are **items on shelves** attached with **putty?**	O	O

PREPARE. SURVIVE. RECOVER.

A little preparation will help you survive the next earthquake and recover faster.

Simple steps to save you money during preparation and how-to videos can be found at **www.totallyunprepared.com.**

This checklist contains a partial list of tips from USGS publication "Putting Down Roots" and Cal EMA website. Earthquake insurance information provided by the CEA.

PROTECT YOURSELF

	Yes	No
Do you have a personal emergency kit with **shoes, a flashlight, work gloves, and copies of your ID?**	O	O
Are your **bookcases secured to the wall?**	O	O
Is your **entertainment center secured to the wall?**	O	O

PROTECT YOUR PETS

	Yes	No
Do you have at least a **3 day supply** of pet food?	O	O
Do you have a **carrier or leash?**	O	O
Do you have copies of your pet's **vaccination records?**	O	O

PROTECT YOUR HOME

	Yes	No
Are **flammable or hazardous chemicals** stored on low shelves?	O	O
Do you know where your **water shutoff** is and do you have a **wrench** to do it?	O	O
Do you know where your **gas shutoff** is and do you have a **wrench** to do it?	O	O
Is your **water heater** secured to **wall studs?**	O	O
Does your **water heater** have a **flexible connector?**	O	O
Is your house **bolted to the foundation?**	O	O
Have you **reinforced crawl spaces** to prevent collapse?	O	O
Home and renters insurance does not cover earthquakes. Do you know how much earthquake insurance costs? Get an estimate at **EarthquakeAuthority.com.**	O	O

www.totallyunprepared.com

Earthquake Safety Checklist courtesy of the California Governor's Office of Emergency Services, the California Earthquake Authority, and the California Seismic Safety Commission

Fill out the Family Emergency Plan on the other side of this page. Cut it out and store it in your Family Emergency Supply Kit

► **YOUR FAMILY MAY NOT BE TOGETHER WHEN AN EMERGENCY HAPPENS, SO THINK ABOUT ANSWERING THE FOLLOWING QUESTIONS WHEN MAKING YOUR PLAN:**

How will my family/household get to safe locations in an emergency?

How will my family/household get in touch if cell phone, Internet, or landline doesn't work? (Even if phones work, lines are often overloaded)

How will we tell each other and loved ones in/out of the area that we're safe?

How will family/household get to a meeting place after the emergency?

How will my family/household get emergency alerts and warnings?

What about our pets?

► **EXAMPLES OF MEETING PLACES:**

In neighborhood – mailbox at end of driveway, neighbor's house

Out of neighborhood – library, community center, school, family or friend's home.

► Have regular family meetings to review your emergency plans, communication plans, supplies, and meeting places. Any changes to worksite(s), schools, etc.? Practice regularly to test the plan and to help everyone in the family remember what to do.

► For more forms and information about emergency planning, go to www.ready.gov click on "search" and enter "make a plan".

Family Emergency Plan

Prepare. Plan. Stay Informed.

Make sure your family has a plan in case of an emergency. Before an emergency happens, sit down together and decide how you wil get in contact with each other, where you will go and what you will do in an emergency. Keep a copy of this plan in your emergency supply kit or another safe place where you can access it in the event of a disaster.

Neighborhood Meeting Place: _____   Phone: _____

Out-of-Neighborhood Meeting Place: _____   Phone: _____

Out-of-Town Meeting Place: _____   Phone: _____

Fill out the following information for each family member and keep it up to date.

Name: _____
Date of Birth: _____

Social Security Number: _____
Important Medical Information: _____

Name: _____
Date of Birth: _____

Social Security Number: _____
Important Medical Information: _____

Name: _____
Date of Birth: _____

Social Security Number: _____
Important Medical Information: _____

Name: _____
Date of Birth: _____

Social Security Number: _____
Important Medical Information: _____

Name: _____
Date of Birth: _____

Social Security Number: _____
Important Medical Information: _____

Name: _____
Date of Birth: _____

Social Security Number: _____
Important Medical Information: _____

Write down where your family spends the most time: work, school and other places you frequent. Schools, daycare providers, workplaces and apartment buildings should all have site-specific emergency plans that you and your family need to know about.

Work Location One
Address: _____
Phone: _____
Evacuation Location: _____

School Location One
Address: _____
Phone: _____
Evacuation Location: _____

Work Location Two
Address: _____
Phone: _____
Evacuation Location: _____

School Location Two
Address: _____
Phone: _____
Evacuation Location: _____

Work Location Three
Address: _____
Phone: _____
Evacuation Location: _____

School Location Three
Address: _____
Phone: _____
Evacuation Location: _____

Other place you frequent
Address: _____
Phone: _____
Evacuation Location: _____

Other place you frequent
Address: _____
Phone: _____
Evacuation Location: _____

Name	Telephone Number	Policy Number

 **Ready.**
Prepare. Plan. Stay Informed.

Family Emergency Plan

 **FEMA**

Make sure your family has a plan in case of an emergency. Fill out these cards and give one to each member of your family to make sure they know who to call and where to meet in case of an emergency.

< FOLD HERE >

ADDITIONAL IMPORTANT PHONE NUMBERS & INFORMATION:

Family Emergency Plan

EMERGENCY CONTACT NAME:
TELEPHONE:

OUT-OF-TOWN CONTACT NAME:
TELEPHONE:

NEIGHBORHOOD MEETING PLACE:
TELEPHONE:

OTHER IMPORTANT INFORMATION:

Ready.

DIAL 911 FOR EMERGENCIES

ADDITIONAL IMPORTANT PHONE NUMBERS & INFORMATION:

Family Emergency Plan

EMERGENCY CONTACT NAME:
TELEPHONE:

OUT-OF-TOWN CONTACT NAME:
TELEPHONE:

NEIGHBORHOOD MEETING PLACE:
TELEPHONE:

OTHER IMPORTANT INFORMATION:

Ready.

DIAL 911 FOR EMERGENCIES

< FOLD HERE >

ADDITIONAL IMPORTANT PHONE NUMBERS & INFORMATION:

Family Emergency Plan

EMERGENCY CONTACT NAME:
TELEPHONE:

OUT-OF-TOWN CONTACT NAME:
TELEPHONE:

NEIGHBORHOOD MEETING PLACE:
TELEPHONE:

OTHER IMPORTANT INFORMATION:

Ready.

DIAL 911 FOR EMERGENCIES

ADDITIONAL IMPORTANT PHONE NUMBERS & INFORMATION:

Family Emergency Plan

EMERGENCY CONTACT NAME:
TELEPHONE:

OUT-OF-TOWN CONTACT NAME:
TELEPHONE:

NEIGHBORHOOD MEETING PLACE:
TELEPHONE:

OTHER IMPORTANT INFORMATION:

Ready.

DIAL 911 FOR EMERGENCIES

Fill out the Family Emergency Plan individual cards on the other side of this page. Cut them out and give one to each member of the family for wallets or school/work emergency kits.

NEED MORE COPIES OF CARDS OR PLAN FORMS?

      ▶ make copies of these pages

      ▶ or get other types of forms from the internet

FEMA **ready.gov** – search "family emergency plans" – several different plan forms, lots of planning information

Red Cross **redcross.org** – search: "family disaster plan"

Find the FEMA Family Emergency Plan forms online: www.fema.gov

Thanks to the Federal Emergency Management Agency for the use of these forms.

61710386R00024

Made in the USA
Charleston, SC
26 September 2016